Curious George®
Bedtime Stories

Margret *and* H. A. Rey

Houghton Mifflin Harcourt Publishing Company
Boston   New York

Contents

MARGRET & H.A.REY'S
Curious George
Goes to the Zoo

Written by Cynthia Platt

Illustrated in the style of H. A. Rey by Mary O'Keefe Young

This is George. George is a good little monkey and
always very curious. Today, George was feeling very excited.
The man with the yellow hat was taking him to the zoo!

As they drove, the man explained to George that this wasn't just any zoo that they were going to visit.

"It's called the Wild Animal Park," the man said. "All of the animals roam around freely."

When they arrived, George saw a
huge banner. George looked up at it,
but he could not read the words.

A friendly zookeeper explained.

"It's an extra-special day here at the Wild Animal Park," she said. "It is our baby rhino's first birthday. We are going to have a party for her later on!"

A party! This was going to be a wonderful trip to the zoo.

George tried to walk into the park where the animals were, but the zookeeper stopped him.

"You can't walk in there!" she said.

"To explore this zoo, you have ride in one of our special cars."

She pointed to a huge car that had no roof on it.

Oh, my! What fun this was going to be.

George and his friend climbed onboard and the car drove into the park.

Soon they were in the midst of the Wild Animal Park.

"Look over there!" said the zookeeper. "There's our pride of lions. We have a large family here."

20

George pointed in the other direction. "Yes, George," said the zookeeper.

"I see the giraffes, too. Their tall necks help them eat leaves from the treetops. And there are two ostriches running this way!"

George was happy to be seeing so many amazing animals.

21

The zoo car drove past a small pond. Pink flamingos waded in the water. Their heads bobbed up and down as they walked on spindly legs.

"The flamingos turn pink because they eat so many tiny pink shrimp," said the zookeeper, but George was not listening.

He had never seen flamingos before. He was curious about how those flamingos were moving.

He leaned out the back of the zoo car as far as he could to take a look. But then—oh! What happened?!

First George lost his balance. Then he fell—
kerplunk!—right out of the zoo car. His friend hadn't
noticed that he had fallen. George ran as quickly as a
little monkey could toward the pond.

The flamingos bobbed their heads and lifted their
feet one at a time. It looked like they were dancing.
George danced with them.

Suddenly, the water in the pond started to move. Then a hippo popped its head out from under the water. What a surprise! George stopped dancing to take a look.

The hippo opened its huge mouth as if it were yawning. George opened his mouth wide, too. It was fun to act like the hippo!

Just then, George noticed that something was rustling in the reeds near the pond. George was curious. He wanted to see what was there.

In an instant, he jumped over to the reeds. He poked his nose inside and saw . . . a baby rhino!

The tiny rhino was cute, but she looked a little
bit sad and a little bit lonely.

George wanted to make that baby rhino feel happy again. He thought and thought. Maybe the baby rhino would like the flamingo dance.

He jumped and bobbed his head and danced his feet up and down.

The baby rhino peeked her head out of the reeds so that she could watch. George danced more, and the rhino walked out of the reeds. She was curious, too!

They were having so much fun that George didn't notice what was behind him.

The zookeeper stomped over to George. She did not look happy. The man with the yellow hat was running behind her.

"You are a naughty little monkey," said the zookeeper. "You were supposed to stay in the car. You and your friend will have to go now."

George walked to the man's side. He waved goodbye to the baby rhino. The man and the zookeeper turned to see whom George was waving to.

"The baby rhino! Why, we've been looking for her all day," said the zookeeper. "She got separated from her mother."

George was glad to see the zookeeper looking happy again. He and the man started walking toward the exit.

The zookeeper ran to stop them. "Thank you for finding our baby rhino, George. And just in time for her birthday party. Will you join us for some cake?"

George jumped with glee. He had forgotten about the party, and he did love cake.

The man and George followed the zookeeper and the baby rhino back to zoo headquarters. The rhino's mother was waiting there for her.

33

The zookeeper brought out a special birthday cake that was shaped like a rhino. George had never seen a cake like that before.

"You can have the first piece, George," said the zookeeper. "I also have a special treat, just for you!" She placed a bunch of bananas in front of him.

George was very happy to have a tasty banana, but he saved room for some cake, too!

MARGRET & H.A. REY'S
Curious George's
and the Firefighters

Illustrated in the style of H. A. Rey by Anna Grossnickle Hines

This is George.
He was a good little monkey and always very curious.
Today George and his friend the man with the yellow hat
joined Mrs. Gray and her class on their field trip to the fire station.

The Fire Chief was waiting for them right next to a big red fire truck.
"Welcome!" he said, and he led everyone upstairs to begin their tour.

There was a kitchen with a big table, and there were snacks for everyone. The Fire Chief told them all about being a firefighter. George tried hard to pay attention, but there were so many things for a little monkey to explore. Like that shiny silver pole in the corner . . .

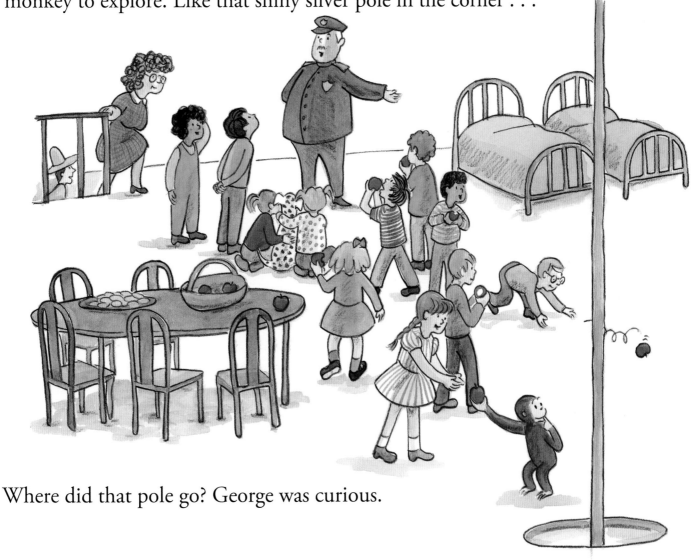

Where did that pole go? George was curious.

Why, it went back downstairs! There was the great big fire truck. There was a map of the city. And there was a whole wall full of coats and hats and big black boots!

George had an idea.
First he stepped into a
pair of boots.

Next, he picked out a helmet.

And, finally, George put on a jacket.
He was a firefighter!

Suddenly . . . *BRRRIINNGG!*

The firefighters all rushed in.

"This is not my helmet!" said one.

"My boots are too big!" said another.

"Hurry! Hurry!" called the Fire Chief. A bright red light on the map of the city told him just where the fire was. There was no time to waste!

One by one, the firefighters jumped into the fire truck.

And so did George.

The fire truck with
all the firefighters sped
out of the firehouse.
And so did George!
The siren screamed and the lights flashed.

The truck turned right. Then it turned left.
   WHOO WHOO WHOO went the whistle,
   and George held on tight.

And just like that the fire truck and all the firefighters pulled up to a pizza parlor on Main Street. Smoke was coming out a window in the back and a crowd was gathering in the street.

"Thank goodness you're here!" cried the cook.

The firefighters rushed off the truck and started
unwinding their hoses. They knew just what to do.
And George was ready to help.
He climbed up on the hose reel . . .

One of the firefighters saw George trying to help, and he took George by the arm and led him out of the way.

"A fire is no place for a monkey!" he said to George. "You stay here where it's safe."

George felt terrible.

George sat on the bench and looked around.
Next to him on the ground was a bucket
full of balls. George reached in and took
one out. It fit in his hand just
right, like the apple
he'd had for a snack.

49

A little girl was watching
George. He tried to give her the
ball, but she was too frightened.

George took
another ball.

And another.
    "Look," a boy said.
"That monkey is juggling!"

The boy took a ball from the cage and
tossed it to George, but it went too high.

George climbed up onto the
fire truck to get it.

Now George had four balls to juggle. He threw the balls higher and higher. He juggled with his hands. He juggled with his feet. He could do all kinds of tricks!

The boy threw another ball to George. George threw a ball back to the boy. The little girl reached down and picked up a ball, too. Soon all the children were throwing and catching, back and forth.

The Fire Chief came to tell everyone that the fire was out. Just then, the little girl laughed and said, "Look, Mommy—a fire monkey!"

"Hey!" called the Fire Chief. "What are you doing up there?"

"What a wonderful idea," the little girl's mother said to the Fire Chief. "Bringing this brave little monkey to help children when they're frightened."

"Oh," the Fire Chief said. "Well, er, thank you."

Before long the fire truck was back at the fire house, where a familiar voice called, "George!" It was the man with the yellow hat.

"This little monkey had quite an adventure," said one of the firefighters.

"Is everyone all right?" asked Mrs. Gray.

"Yes, it was just a small fire," said the Fire Chief.
"And George was a big help."
Now the field trip was coming to an end.
But there was one more treat in store . . .

All the children got to take a ride around the neighborhood on the shiny red fire truck, and they each got their very own fire helmet. Even George! And it was just the right size for a brave little monkey.

MARGRET & H. A. REY'S
Curious George
at the Aquarium

Written by R. P. Anderson

Illustrated in the style of H. A. Rey by Anna Grossnickle Hines

This is George.

He was a good little monkey and always very curious.

Today George and the man with the yellow hat were visiting the aquarium.

"George," said the man, "please wait here while I buy the tickets."

George tried to wait, but he was so excited! What was inside?

He wanted to look over the walls, but they were too high.

Just then, he heard a *SPLASH!*
and a *WHOOSH!* Water flew high
into the air. People cheered. What
could that be? George was curious.

He hopped over the gate into the aquarium. How surprised he was!

Swimming right in front of George were two beluga whales!
The mother and baby beluga whale swam right past him.

And not far away was a family of sea lions, diving and splashing. What fun!

George noticed people walking toward a big door—could there be more to see? He followed the crowd.

Now where was he? It was darker
inside and there were fish everywhere!
George did not know where to look first.

In one tank there were
sharp-toothed piranhas,

in another tank there
were sea horses,

and in another tank there
was a large red octopus!

George saw a group of children across the room. An aquarium staff member was pointing to different sea creatures. "This is a starfish, this is a clam, and this is an urchin."

Nearby, there was a long, low, colorful tank. It was perfect for touching!

70

George was curious. As he reached his hand into the water, a large crab came scuttling out from under a rock and right toward his finger!

Snap!

Ouch!

Poor George. He did not like this exhibit.

George slipped out a door into the sunlight. But, oh! What was going on here?

George saw fat, funny-looking black and white fish flying under the water. As he watched they flew up out of the water. What kind of fish does that, and where did they go? George wondered.

Where Penguins Live

George climbed up and into their exhibit.

They were not fish at all, but penguins, of course!

George hopped like a penguin,

flapped his wings like a penguin,

and waddled like a penguin.

A crowd gathered and laughed.
But when he slid on his belly like a penguin . . .

The aquarium staff stopped by to check on the penguins.

"A monkey! In the penguin exhibit?"

George opened a door to escape, but instead . . . all the penguins ran out! Penguins, penguins everywhere!

The staff was angry at George. How could they catch all the penguins?

In all the excitement nobody noticed the penguin chick falling into the water! No one but George.

The baby penguin hadn't learned to swim yet. As only a monkey can, George scaled the rope hanging over the beluga tank and swung over the water, saving the chick.

The director of the aquarium and the man with the yellow hat heard the commotion and came running.

"That monkey helped the baby penguin," said a boy in the crowd.

"No one else could have saved him," said a girl.

The director thanked George for his help and made him an honorary staff member of the aquarium.

George said goodbye to his new penguin friends. He could not wait to come back to the aquarium and visit them again!

MARGRET & H.A. REY'S
Curious George's
Dinosaur Discovery

Written by Catherine Hapka

Illustrated in the style of H. A. Rey by Anna Grossnickle Hines

This is George.

He was a good little monkey and always very curious.

George loved to go places with his friend the man with the yellow hat. One of their favorite places to visit was the Dinosaur Museum.

"Today is a special day," George's friend said. "We are going to do something very interesting!"

George was curious. What could be more interesting than a trip to the Dinosaur Museum?

The man with the yellow hat led the way through the museum.
George wanted to stop and look at the dinosaur bones. But his friend
kept going, so George kept following.

Finally they walked right out the back door!

A van was waiting for them outside. "Climb in, George," said the man with the yellow hat.

George looked out the window as the van drove off. Where could they be going?

At last, the van reached a rocky quarry. Dozens of people were there. Some were digging with shovels. Others were using pickaxes or other kinds of tools.

"Surprise!" George's friend said. "We're going to help the museum scientists dig for dinosaur bones!"

George was curious. Were there really dinosaurs buried in the quarry? He ran over for a better look. "Hello," said a friendly scientist. "Are you here to help with the dig?"

George watched the
scientist work. She dug up
some dirt and put it into
her sifting pan.

It took a long time to sift it.
And in the end—no dinosaur
bones!

"Oh, well," she said. "Time
to try again!"

But the next pan was empty, too. So was the next one. And the one after that.

George yawned. So far digging for dinosaurs was not as exciting as he'd expected.

George was curious. Could he help to find dinosaur bones?

He found a spare shovel lying nearby. He dug and dug.
But he didn't find any dinosaurs.

When he climbed out of his hole, George spotted another scientist.
He was dusting something with a small brush.

"Oh, well," the scientist said. "It's not a bone. Just a rock."

George wanted to help. He picked up
a brush and went to work.

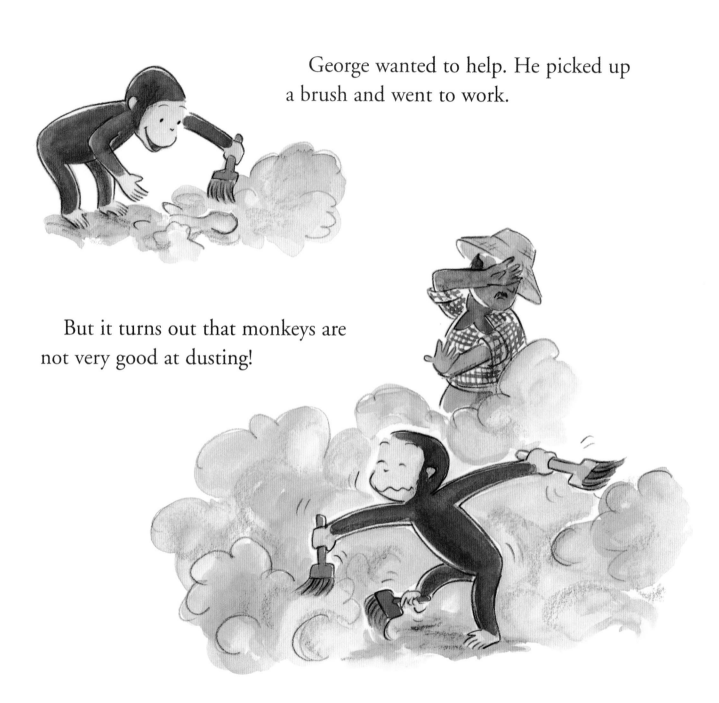

But it turns out that monkeys are
not very good at dusting!

As he hurried away from the cloud of dust, George bumped into a wheelbarrow. Maybe there were dinosaur bones in it!

He climbed up to look inside. But the wheelbarrow was awfully tippy . . .

CRASH!

George, the wheelbarrow, and a whole lot of dirt went flying.
"Hey!" someone cried. "What's that monkey doing?"

George scampered away, straight up the cliff. Monkeys are good at climbing, so George kept going — higher and higher.

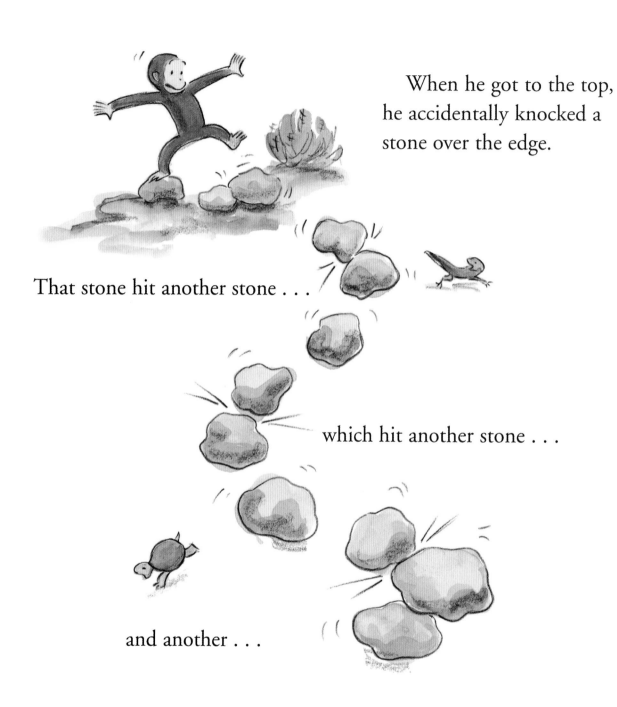

When he got to the top,
he accidentally knocked a
stone over the edge.

That stone hit another stone . . .

which hit another stone . . .

and another . . .

Oh, no! It was a rockslide!

The man with the yellow hat called for George to come down. George wanted to climb down, but he was afraid the scientists would be angry with him.

But the scientists didn't look angry.

"Look!" one cried, pointing. "Look what that monkey just uncovered!"

George could hardly believe what he saw. Dinosaur bones!

After that, the dinosaur dig was
even more fun. George helped the
scientists dig . . .

and sift . . .

and dust . . .

and take photographs of
the bones he had found.

And the next time he and the man with the yellow hat visited the Dinosaur Museum, George got to see HIS dinosaur on display!

MARGRET & H. A. REY'S
Curious George's
First Day of School

Illustrated in the style of H. A. Rey by Anna Grossnickle Hines

This is George.

He was a good little monkey and always very curious.

Today George was so excited, he could barely eat his breakfast.
"You have a big day ahead of you, George," said his friend the man
with the yellow hat.

It *was* a big day for George. It was the first day of school, and he had been invited to be a special helper.

George and his friend walked together to the schoolyard. Some of the children were nervous, but George could not wait for the fun to begin.

In the classroom George's friend introduced him to Mr. Apple.
"Thank you for inviting George to school today," the man with the
yellow hat said to the teacher. Then he waved goodbye. "Have a good
day, George. I'll be back to pick you up after school."

The children were excited to have a monkey in class. "George is going to be our special helper," Mr. Apple told them.

And what a helper he was!
At story time George held
the book.

At math time the
children could count
on George.

And at recess George made sure
everyone had a ball . . .

and a well-balanced snack.

After lunch Mr. Apple got out paints and brushes. George saw red, yellow, and blue paint. Three colors were not very many. George was curious. Could he help make more colors?

First George mixed red and blue to make . . .

purple.

Next George mixed red and yellow to make . . .

orange.

Then George mixed
yellow and blue to make . . .

green.

Finally George mixed all
the colors to make . . .

117

. . . a big mess!

The children thought the mess was funny. But Mr. Apple did not.

"Oh, dear," he said. "We are going to need something to clean this up. Everyone please sit quietly while I look."

George did not mean to make such a mess and he certainly did not want to sit quietly. He wanted to help—it was his job, after all. George had an idea.

In the
hallway
George
found
a closet.
In the
closet
he found
a bucket.
In the bucket
he found just
what he needed . . .

121

A mop!

George was on his way back to the classroom when he heard somebody yell.

"Stop! Stop! What are you doing with my mop?" The janitor ran after George.

"Stop! Stop! No running in the halls!" The principal ran after the janitor.

But George was going too fast to stop. He grabbed the doorway and swung inside, and . . .

S
P
L
O
S
H
!

The bucket tipped,
the mop dropped,
and George slid
across the floor.

Now the mess was even bigger.

Mr. Apple looked surprised. The principal frowned. The janitor just shook his head.

And George—poor George. He felt terrible. Maybe he was not such a good helper after all.

The children felt terrible too. They did not like to see George looking so sad. They thought he was a great helper. Now they wanted to help him.

So the children all lent a hand (and some feet).

And before anyone knew it, the mess was gone!

"That little monkey sure is helpful," the janitor said.

"It looks like Mr. Apple has a whole class full of helpers," the principal added.

At the end of the day, when George's friend arrived to pick him up, Mr. Apple said, "Thank you for all of your help, George. We hope you will come help us again."

The children cheered. They hoped George would come again too.

George waved goodbye to his new friends. What a great day it had been! He could not wait to come back to school.

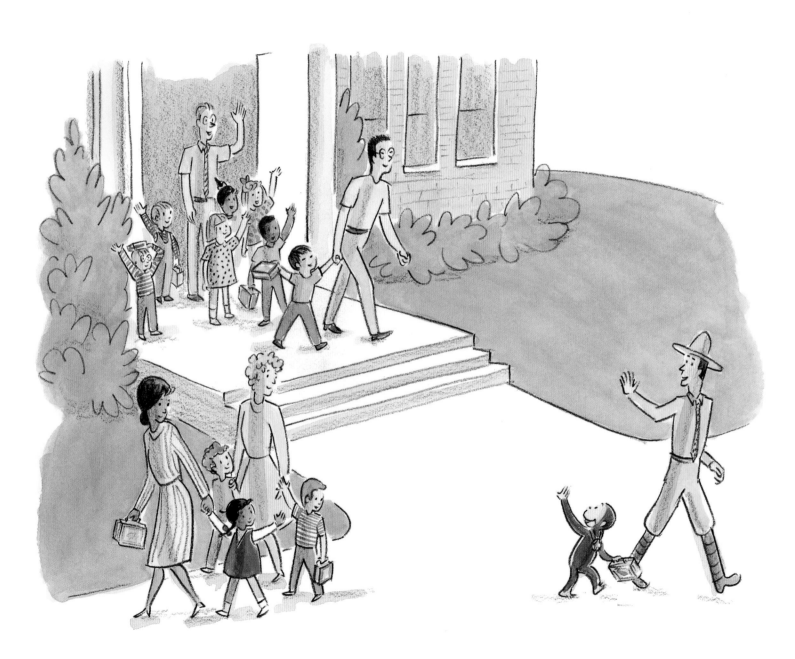

MARGRET & H.A.REY'S
Curious George
and the Puppies

Illustrated in the style of H. A. Rey by Vipah Interactive

This is George.

George was a good little monkey and always very curious.

One day George went for a walk with his friend, the man with the yellow hat.

When they sat down to rest, they noticed a tiny kitten peeking out from under a bush. The kitten looked frightened.

"Perhaps she is lost," said the man with the yellow hat.

Together, he and George searched the park for the little kitten's owner.

But the kitten was all alone.

"This kitten is too young to be on her own," the man said. "We should take her to the animal shelter, where they can care for her and find her a home."

So George and the kitten and the man with the yellow hat drove to the animal shelter.

The director of the shelter was glad to see them. "It was good of you to bring the kitten here," she said. "We will be happy to take care of her."

George gave the kitten to the director, then he and the man with the yellow hat walked inside.

"Come in," the director said, "but watch where you step. We have a large litter of puppies and one has gotten out of his cage. We're still looking for him, so please be careful."

She closed the door quickly behind them.

George had never been to an animal shelter before. Animals of all kinds were being cared for here. George saw bunnies, cats, turtles, and guinea pigs. He even saw a snake.

But he didn't see any puppies.

"George, I need to sign some papers," said the man with
the yellow hat. "Please stay here and don't be too curious."

Just as the man with the yellow hat
left the room, George heard barking.
Maybe it was the puppies!

But where was it coming from?

George was curious.

He followed the
barking noises . . .

and found a room full of dogs! There were yellow dogs, spotted dogs, sleek dogs, and fluffy dogs. There were quiet dogs and yappy dogs and even a dog without a tail. But where were the puppies?

Then George saw a
little wagging tail.

Then another.

And another!

Once George saw the
puppies, he could not take
his eyes off them.

He had to pet one.

Here was a puppy!
The puppy liked George.

George wanted to hold the
puppy. Slowly, he opened the
door . . .

but before George could even reach the puppy, the mother dog
pushed the door open and was off like a shot! George tried to close
the door after her, but the puppies were too fast!

There was nothing George could do.

Puppies were everywhere!

Puppies hid under the desk. Puppies barked at bunnies. One puppy played with a telephone cord and another climbed on top of a cage to watch the others get into mischief.

Soon all the dogs were barking, the cats were meowing, and the bunnies rustled into the corner of their cage.

147

"Oh no!" cried the director as she and the man with the yellow hat rushed into the room. "Now ALL the puppies are out!"

The man with the yellow hat helped the director gather up the puppies and put them safely back in their cage. Soon all the animals settled down and were quiet.

Except for one.
Who was still barking?
It was the mother dog!
What was she barking at? There was nothing here but a door.

There must be something on the
other side, thought George.

He opened the door.

It was the missing puppy! Everyone was happy to finally find the puppy. The director scooped him up and said, "George, you certainly caused a ruckus! But if you hadn't let the puppies out, we might still be searching for this little one."

Then she gave the puppies and their mother a snack.

"These puppies are now big enough to go live with families who will take care of them," she said. "Do you want to take one home with you, George?"

George did.

MARGRET & H.A.REY'S
Curious George
and the Pizza Party

Written by Cynthia Platt
Illustrated in the style of H. A. Rey by Mary O'Keefe Young

George was a good little monkey and always very curious.
Today, he wasn't just curious—he was excited. So excited,
in fact, that he was turning flips and standing on his head!

A little girl in George's building had invited him to
her pizza party. George had never been to a pizza party
before, but he loved parties and he loved pizza, so he
knew it had to be good.

"George, it's time for the pizza party," said the man with the yellow hat.

"Have fun—and remember to be on your best behavior!"

George got to the party in perfect time!

"Hi, George," called out the little girl. But oh, what was all of this? The children were wearing puffy white chef's hats and checkered aprons.

George got a hat and an apron, too! The best was yet to come.
They weren't just going to eat pizza. They were going to make
it, too.

  "Everyone will get a piece of pizza dough to roll out and make
a special pizza," explained the girl's mother. There were many
little lumps of dough.

  "But first, let's play some games!" she said.

Everyone went into the living room to play pin the pepperoni on the pizza. Everyone, that is, except George. He was curious about those pieces of dough.

George thought and thought. If lots of little pieces of dough were good, maybe one huge one would be even better.

He gathered the lumps of dough together and
squished and squashed them until they became the
very biggest piece of dough he'd ever seen. What fun!
Maybe rolling it out would be even more fun!

George poured flour out on the table, and he rolled and rolled and rolled the dough with a rolling pin.

It was messy work!
First he bumped over
one of the chairs.

Crash!

Then he knocked over the sack of flour. *Thump!*

The flour looked like snow lying on the floor of the kitchen.
George liked snow, though, so he didn't mind at all.
Soon he had gotten the dough nice and thin.

But the thinner it got, the farther it spread out.
Before he knew it, the dough covered the
table . . . then the chairs . . . and then George.

Without the flour, it started to stick to everything—including George!
George stopped to think.

Maybe the dough was better off in small pieces after all.

167

George got a pair of scissors and began cutting
up the dough into lots of different shapes.
He thought everyone would be pleased.

"George! What have you done to the kitchen?"
The little girl's mother didn't look very happy.
"I think it's time for you to go home now."
How surprised and sad George was.

Just then, the children burst into the kitchen and saw the mess that George had made.

"George, what happened?" asked one boy. The other children looked at the shapes George had made with wide eyes.

"Wow, George! I've never seen pizza dough like that before," said the little girl, smiling.

"Well," said her mother, "if you can clean up this mess quickly, George, I suppose you can still stay to make pizza."

The children all helped George clean the kitchen.
He was lucky to have so many good friends.
As they worked, they talked about the pizza!
"I'm going to make a pizza that looks like a star,"
said one little boy.
"And I'm going to make one that looks like
a house!" said a girl.

Once the kitchen was clean, the real fun began!
All of the children picked out perfect pieces of
dough and got to work.

They spooned on tomato sauce and sprinkled on cheese.
They added lots of vegetables and pepperoni.

The pizzas looked wonderful! One looked like a rainbow,
another like a stop sign, and still another like a balloon.
There was even a pizza that looked curiously like George!

"Well, George," said the little girl's mother, "the pizzas taste great, and thanks to you, they look wonderful, too!"

Everyone agreed. It was the best pizza anyone had ever seen—or tasted!

For the second time that day, George was so
happy that he turned flips and stood on his head.

Of course, it was a little harder to turn flips with so
much pizza in his belly. But George didn't mind.
It had been a wonderful pizza party!

MARGRET & H.A.REY'S

Curious George
at the Baseball Game

Written by Laura Driscoll

Illustrated in the style of H. A. Rey by Anna Grossnickle Hines

This is George.

He was a good little monkey and always very curious.

Today George and the man with the yellow hat were going to the ballpark to watch a baseball game. George couldn't wait to see what it would be like.

At the baseball stadium, the man with the yellow hat introduced George to his friend, the head coach of the Mudville Miners. He had arranged for George to watch the game from the dugout. What a treat! George got a Miners cap to wear. Then he sat on the bench with the players. He felt just like part of the team!

The players cheered a Miners home run. George cheered, too.

The players groaned at a Miners strikeout. George groaned, too.

Then George noticed one of the Miners coaches making funny motions with his hands. He touched his cap. He pinched his nose. He dusted off his shoulder.

Hmm, thought George. Maybe this was another way to cheer on the team.

So George made some hand
motions, too. He tugged at his ear.

He rubbed his tummy.

He scratched his chin.

Just then, a Miners player got tagged out at second base. The player pointed at George. "That monkey!" he said. "He distracted me with his funny signs."

Oops! The coach had been giving directions to the base runner. George's hand signals had taken his mind off the play. Poor George! He had only been trying to be part of the team. Instead the Miners had lost a chance to score.

George watched the rest of the game from a stadium seat. Or at least he *tried* to watch the game. There was so much going on around him.

There was food for sale.

There were shouting fans.

There was a woman holding a big camera . . .

189

The woman pointed her camera at some fans. And look! Those fans waved out from the huge screen on the ballpark scoreboard.

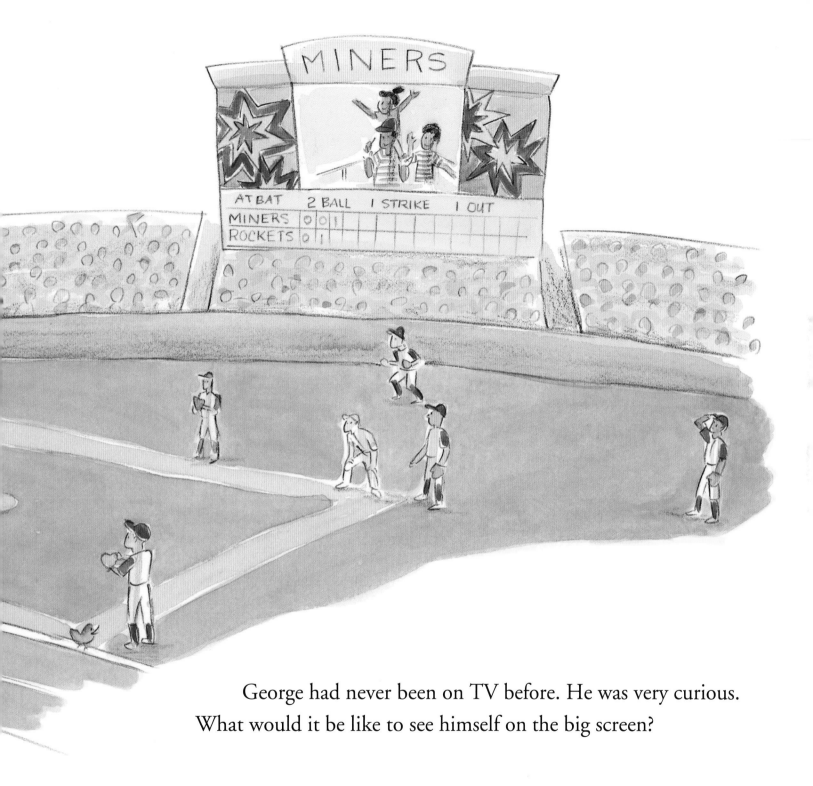

George had never been on TV before. He was very curious.
What would it be like to see himself on the big screen?

He soon learned the answer: it was exciting!

George liked seeing himself on the screen.

"Hey, you!" shouted the camerawoman. "Cut that out!"

Uh-oh! George had gotten a little carried away. He ran off, with the angry camerawoman hot on his heels.

In the busy stadium breezeway, George hid behind a popcorn cart. He waited for the camerawoman to pass by.

Just then, George heard a noise behind him. It was a quiet little noise—like a sigh, or a sniff. What could have made that noise? George wondered.

George turned. There, behind the cart, was a little boy, crying.
George wanted to help. He crept out of his hiding place and over to
the boy.

"Ah-ha! There you are!" shouted the camerawoman, spotting George. Then the camerawoman noticed the teary-eyed boy. She seemed to forget that she was mad at George.

"I'm lost," the boy said. "I can't find my dad."

If only there were a way to let the boy's dad know where he was. But there *was* a way! The camerawoman aimed her lens at the little boy, and . . .

there he was on the big screen for everyone to see—including his dad.

Within minutes, the boy and his father were together again and the man with the yellow hat had come to find George.

"I can't thank you enough," the boy's father said to the camerawoman.

The camerawoman shrugged. "Don't thank me," she said. She patted George on the back. "It was this little fellow who found your son."

George was the star of the day.

MARGRET & H.A.REY'S
Curious George
at the Parade

Illustrated in the style of H. A. Rey by Vipah Interactive

This is George.

He was a good little monkey and always very curious.

Today George and his friend, the man with the yellow hat, were in the city for the big holiday parade.

They found a place in the crowd, but an announcement had just been made.

"The parade may not start for a while, George," the man said. "The wind is too strong for the big balloons. Let's go in this department store while we wait."

George and his friend looked around the store as they waited for the wind to settle down. Suddenly, something strange caught George's eye. What could it be? He was curious.

But when George looked out the window,

he didn't see anything strange. He saw the parade! He saw floats, clowns, and jugglers, and a band standing in straight rows. Then George thought he saw an elephant eating a treat.

That made George hungry.
(It had been a long time since
breakfast.) Now he could think
only of finding a snack.

Why, here was a treat just
like what he ate in the jungle:
fresh nuts — right off the tree!

George was lucky to be a
monkey...

he simply climbed out the window
and jumped into the tree!

Then he pulled and pulled. But
the nuts would not come off the
tree. They were not so fresh after all.
In fact, they were not even real. But
George did not know that.

He pulled harder and harder. The
tree began to sway...

Suddenly, there was a loud *SNAP!*

Then, *CRASH!*
Down came the tree.
Down came George.
And down came all the nuts!

Luckily, George was not hurt. But still he did not have a snack.

He raced after the nuts. He chased them around the elephant and under the clown, then in and out of the band's straight rows. "My perfect rows!" the bandleader cried. "You've ruined my perfect rows!"

The bandleader raced after George. He chased him down the street and around the corner, but he was not quick enough.

Where was George?

Soon the bandleader tired of searching and went back to straighten his rows. He did not know where the little monkey had gone— George was nowhere to be found.

George was not sure where he had gone either — and the nuts were nowhere to be found. After all that, George had lost his snack. After all that, George had lost his way. Now how would he get back to the department store and back to the man with the yellow hat?

Just then a bus was stopping at the corner. George liked to ride the bus. Maybe it could take him back to his friend. Quickly, he hopped on the bus and away they went.

From his seat up on top,
George could see everything.
The bus rounded a corner.
Here was something familiar!

But something was wrong. Two balloons had drifted off course—
their ropes were tangled. The parade helpers were trying to fix them
and a crowd gathered to watch. As the bus came to a stop, someone

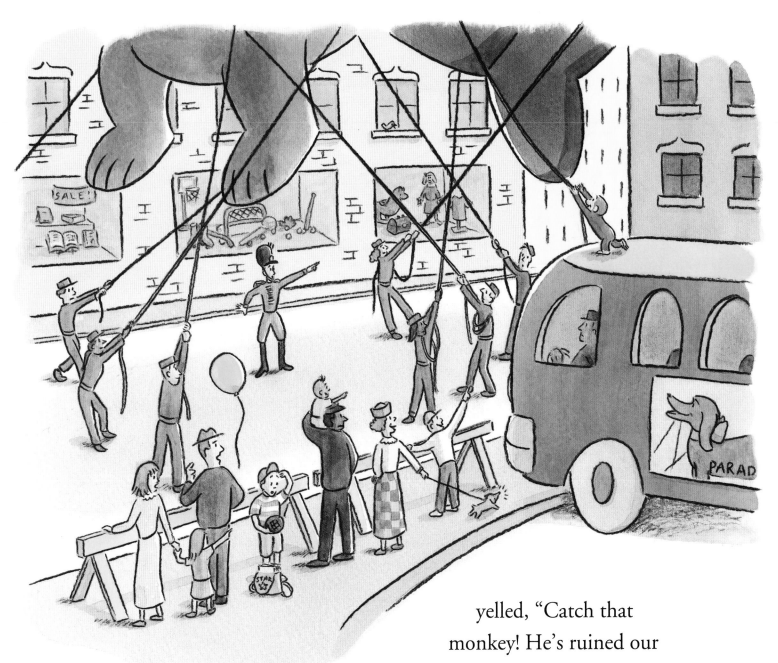

yelled, "Catch that monkey! He's ruined our parade!" It was the bandleader, and he was pointing right at George!

George did not want to be caught, but there was no way for him to get down. There was only one way to go...

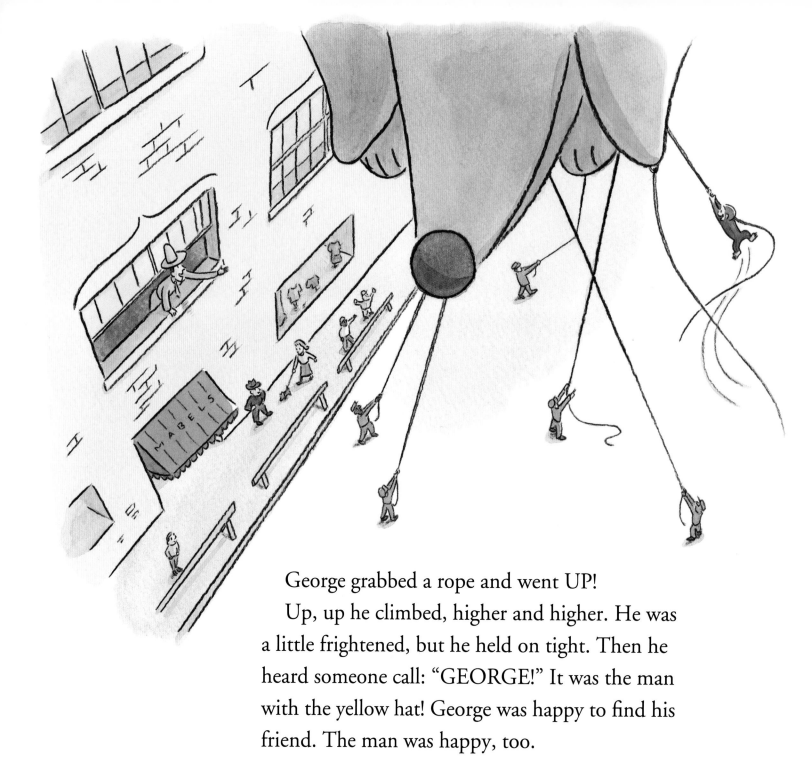

George grabbed a rope and went UP!

Up, up he climbed, higher and higher. He was a little frightened, but he held on tight. Then he heard someone call: "GEORGE!" It was the man with the yellow hat! George was happy to find his friend. The man was happy, too.

George swung from one rope to another. Now he felt like he was in the jungle swinging from vine to vine.

"Look," someone shouted from below. "The little monkey is fixing the balloons!"

223

Then George swung safely into the arms of the man with the yellow hat! The crowd below cheered — the ropes were no longer tangled!

When George and his friend arrived back on the sidewalk, it was time to start the parade.

The bandleader was no longer angry—George was a hero! Even the mayor came to meet George. "I hear you created quite a stir, George," he said. "But at last everything is in order. Would you like to ride with me in the parade?"

Soon the balloons started moving, the music started playing, and the band marched down the street in straight rows.

And there, leading the whole parade, was Curious George.

MARGRET & H.A.REY'S
Curious George
Feeds the Animals

Illustrated in the style of H. A. Rey by Vipah Interactive

This is George.

George was a good little monkey and always very curious.

One day George went to the zoo with his friend, the man with the yellow hat. A new rain forest exhibit was opening and they wanted to be the first ones inside.

But when they got to the new exhibit, the doors were closed. "We'll have to come back later, George," the man said. "Why don't we visit the other animals while we wait?"

First they stopped to watch a zookeeper feed the seals. When he tossed little fish in the air, the seals jumped up to catch them. Then they barked for more.

It looked like fun to feed the animals!

"Would you like something to eat, too, George?" asked the man with the yellow hat, and he bought a snack for them to share.

When they stopped to see the crocodile, George remembered how the zoo-keeper had fed fish to the seals. He was curious. Would the crocodile like something to eat?

George tossed him a treat — and the crocodile snapped it out of the air!

Next they visited the koalas. George thought the koalas were cute.
Here was a friendly one—she was curious, too. She wanted to see
what George was eating, so he held out his hand to share.

George shared his treats with an elephant

and a baby kangaroo.

George was making lots
of new friends at the zoo.
The lion was already eating,
but the hippopotamus tried a
snack. Next he gave a treat
to an ostrich.

236

Then George saw the giraffes.
What fun to feed a giraffe!
Giraffes usually have their heads up high in the trees, but George could see these giraffes would be easy to feed.

But as soon as he held out his hand, a zookeeper came
running. The zookeeper looked angry. Was he angry with George?
George didn't know — and he didn't want to stay to find out.
He slipped away . . .

and the giraffes were happy to help!

But where did George go?

He was trying his best to hide. But little monkeys can't stay still for long. When George wiggled, the zookeeper was waiting. "I see you!" he said.

Just then another zookeeper hurried by. "Come quick!" she yelled. "Someone saw the parrot!"

The first zookeeper led George to a bench.

"The parrot from our new exhibit escaped and I must help find it," he explained.

He told George to wait for him there, and before he left he said, "Don't you know you're not supposed to feed the animals? The wrong food might make them sick."

George felt awful.

He didn't know he wasn't supposed to feed the animals. He didn't want to make them sick.

George was looking at the treat in his hand when all of a sudden,

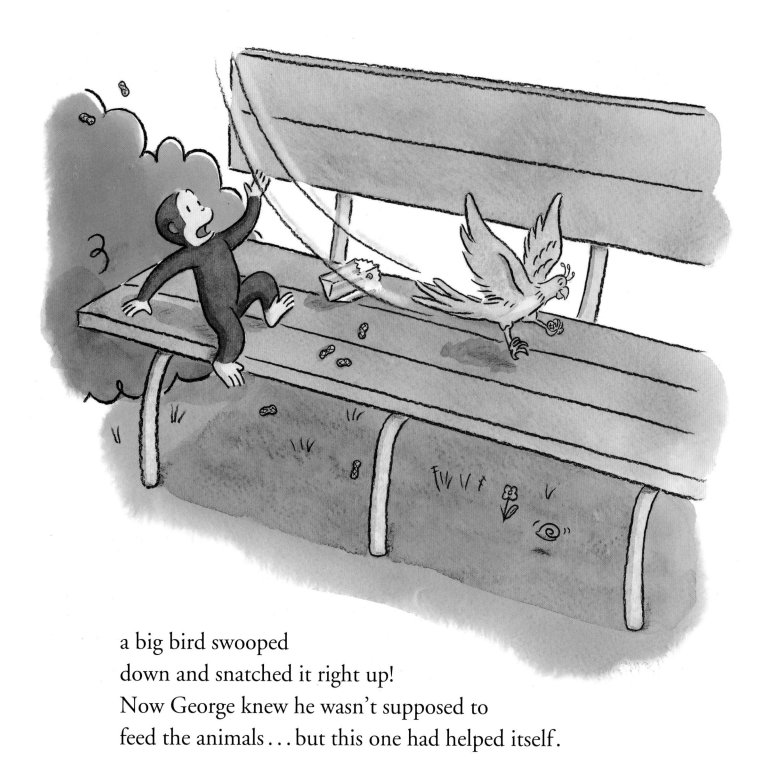

a big bird swooped
down and snatched it right up!
Now George knew he wasn't supposed to
feed the animals ... but this one had helped itself.

A zookeeper passing by was happy to see George. "You found the parrot!" she said. "We've been looking for this bird all day."

When she saw George's snack, she said, "This isn't the best thing to feed a parrot, but a little won't hurt. Would you like to help me put him back where he belongs?"

George was glad to help after all the trouble he had caused, and together they went back to the exhibit.

245

"There's our problem," the zoo-keeper said, pointing to a hole in the netting. As the zookeepers discussed how to fix it, George had an idea. . . .

He climbed up like only a monkey can, and when he reached the hole — he tied the netting back together!

Meanwhile, the first zookeeper returned. "Catch that naughty monkey!" he yelled. "He was feeding the animals!"

"But that little monkey found the parrot," another zookeeper told him. "And look — he fixed the netting. Now we can open the exhibit."

When George came down, all the zookeepers cheered.

Finally the celebration began and the doors were opened. The man with the yellow hat was there, and he and George got to be the first ones inside!

As George walked in, the zookeepers thanked him for all his help. "Please visit anytime!" they said.

George couldn't wait to come back and see his friends. But next time he'd remember, unless you're a zookeeper . . .